For Peter B.

S.P.

For Marie

P.M.

Text copyright © 1993 by Saviour Pirotta
Illustrations copyright © 1993 by Peter Melnyczuk
All rights reserved.

CIP Data is available.

First published in the United States 1993
by Dutton Children's Books,
a division of Penguin Books USA Inc.
375 Hudson Street, New York, New York 10014
Originally published in Great Britain 1993
by J.M. Dent, The Orion Publishing Group, London
Typography by Adrian Leichter
Printed in Italy
First American Edition
ISBN 0-525-45125-0
1 3 5 7 9 10 8 6 4 2

*The illustrations for this book were prepared
using colored inks, pencils, and pastels.*

FOLLOW THAT CAT!

by **Saviour Pirotta**

pictures by **Peter Melnyczuk**

DUTTON CHILDREN'S BOOKS • NEW YORK

Cassie and Mike were best friends. They did everything together. When Mike went to visit his Uncle Linus, Cassie went too.

That's where Cassie met Pumpkin, Uncle Linus's large, striped cat. He had golden eyes and long whiskers.

As the children stroked Pumpkin, Uncle Linus told them about his unusual house. "Did you know it has three doors? A front door, a back door, and a secret door."

"A secret door?" said Cassie. "Where does it lead to?"

Uncle Linus didn't answer. Instead he held up a jar full of colored keys.

"If you use this gray key," he said, "it just leads into a closet. But if you use another color, it can take you any-where."

Cassie and Mike stared at the jar in amazement.

"Can we try one now?" they begged.

"Just the gray key. I'll put your coats away, but then I have to go to the store before it closes. I won't be long," Uncle Linus said.

He took a key from the jar, opened the closet, and quickly put their coats inside. A fishy smell wafted out. Pumpkin sniffed hungrily and slipped through the doorway.

Uncle Linus was in such a hurry that he didn't notice. He closed the door, dropped the key back into the jar, and left.

"I wonder where Pumpkin is?" Cassie asked a moment
later.

"I think I saw him go into the closet," said Mike, "but I
never saw him come out."

Mike opened the door with the gray key, but Pumpkin
was not inside. "Where could he have gone?" Cassie cried.

"Remember what Uncle Linus said about the other
keys?" Mike asked. "Maybe he used the wrong key, and
the door opened to someplace else!"

There were four keys left in the jar. "Will your uncle be
angry if we try another one?" Cassie asked.

"He would want us to find Pumpkin," Mike said. He took
the green key and opened the door again.

"Come on!" Cassie shouted as she stepped into a lush, green country where sparkling water tumbled in streams and huge birds soared in the cloudless sky.

"Excuse me," said Mike to two women who were picking tea leaves. "Have you seen a large, striped cat?"

"We have," they replied. "Come with us."

Cassie and Mike followed the tea pickers.

"Look," one of them said. "There is your beast."

The children looked at the cat lying in the shade. It was huge and striped, but it wasn't Pumpkin.

"That's a tiger!" Mike gasped, feeling scared and excited at the same time. "A real, live tiger."

The children thanked the tea pickers and hurried back to the secret door.

"Let's try the yellow key," Cassie said.

Mike opened the door, and a hot, dry breeze blew into the room. They stepped into a golden land full of tall trees with whispering leaves. Their skin tingled from the burning sun.

"Have you seen a cat with golden eyes?" Cassie asked the two men who walked across the dusty plain to greet them.

"Yes, we have," they said. "We'll show you where he is."

They led the children past rhinos and a herd of giraffes drinking at a river.

"There he is," the men said, pointing ahead.

"That isn't our cat," Cassie gulped, hardly daring to breathe. "That's a lion."

They raced back to the secret door.

"We can't give up," Cassie said. "Try the white key."

As Mike opened the door, a flurry of snow filled the room. Holding hands, the children clambered up an icy mountain.

"Good afternoon," called a man riding a yak.

"Good afternoon," said Cassie. "Have you seen a cat with long whiskers?"

"Yes, I have," said the man. "He's in that cave."

A big cat padded out of the opening.

"That's not Pumpkin," the children gasped as they hid behind a rock for safety. "That's a snow leopard."

And they dashed back to the secret door.

"There's only the blue key left," Cassie said as she opened the door.

A fishy smell wafted out. Mike tiptoed after Cassie and found himself riding on blue waves in a sailing ship.

"Have you seen a striped cat with golden eyes and long whiskers?" he asked the sailor.

"I have indeed," the captain replied.

"Oh, I hope it's Pumpkin," Cassie said. "Where is he?"

"Some of the crew took him ashore in our dinghy," the captain said. "We can follow them, if you like."

"Oh, yes," said Cassie and Mike together.

As they sailed closer to shore, Mike could see a cat
standing on the prow of the boat ahead.

"It *is* Pumpkin!" he cried, pointing.

"Hooray!" Cassie shouted.

The boats reached the harbor. Pumpkin leaped ashore.

"Follow him, quick!" Mike said.

Pumpkin sped past the warehouses on the seafront and
disappeared down a narrow alleyway. The children ran
after him.

Pumpkin turned a corner.

"I know this street," Mike said.

Pumpkin raced past the stores.

"I know these stores," Mike cried.

Pumpkin turned another corner.

"This is our street," Mike said.

"And that's your Uncle Linus's house," said Cassie, nearly out of breath.

The children followed Pumpkin into the house. They found him in the kitchen drinking milk. He finished, licked his striped coat, and cleaned his long whiskers. Then he blinked his golden eyes and purred happily.

Cassie and Mike told Uncle Linus what had happened.

"Well, you've had quite an adventure, but you shouldn't have worried about Pumpkin," Uncle Linus said, smiling. "Cats always find their own way home."